9x7

E
Marshall, James, 1942-
George and Martha rise and
shine.
Houghton, 1976
46 p. : ill. ;

C

GEORGE AND MARTHA

RISE AND SHINE

GEORGE AND MARTHA RISE AND SHINE

JAMES MARSHALL

HOUGHTON MIFFLIN COMPANY BOSTON

FOR MY FATHER

Library of Congress Cataloging in Publication Data

Marshall, James, 1942-
  George and Martha rise and shine.

  SUMMARY: Five brief episodes about two friends,
George and Martha, who happen to be hippopotamuses.
  1. Friendship--Fiction. 2. Hippopotamus--Fiction.
3. Short Stories I. Title
PZ7.M35672Ge   E   76-14350
ISBN 0-395-24738-1 RNF ISBN 0-395-28006-0 PAP

RNF Y PAP Y 10 9 8 7 6 5 4 3

ABOUT TWO FINE FRIENDS

~

STORY NUMBER ONE
THE FIBBER

One day George wanted to impress Martha.

"I used to be a champion jumper," he said.

Martha raised an eyebrow.

"And," said George, "I used to be a wicked pirate."

"Hmmm," said Martha.

George tried harder. "Once I was even
a famous snake charmer!"

"Oh, goody," said Martha.

Martha went to the closet and got out Sam.

"Here's a snake for you to charm."

"Eeeek," cried George.

And he jumped right out of his chair.

"It's only a toy *stuffed* snake," said Martha. "I'm
surprised a famous snake charmer is such a scaredy-cat."
"I told some fibs," said George.
"For shame," said Martha.
"But you can see what a good jumper I am," said George.
"That's true," said Martha.

STORY NUMBER TWO

THE EXPERIMENT

Martha was in her laboratory.

"What are you doing?" asked George.

"I'm studying fleas," said Martha.

"Cute little critters," said George.

"You don't understand," said Martha.

"This is serious. This is science."

The next day, George noticed that Martha
was scratching a lot. She looked
uncomfortable.

George bought Martha some special soap. After
her shower Martha felt much better.

"I think I'll stop studying fleas," said Martha.

"Good idea," said George.

"I think I'll study bees instead," said Martha.

"Oh dear," said George.

STORY NUMBER 3

THE PICNIC

One Saturday morning, George wanted to sleep late.

"I love sleeping late," said George.

But Martha had other ideas.

She wanted to go on a picnic.

"Here she comes!" said George to himself.

Martha did her best to get George out of bed.

"Picnic time!" sang Martha.

But George didn't budge.

Martha played a tune on her saxophone.

George put little balls of cotton in his ears and pulled up the covers.

Martha tickled George's toes.

"Stop it!" said George.

"Picnic time!" sang Martha.

"But I'm *not* going on a picnic!" said George.

"Oh yes you *are*!" said his friend.

Martha had a clever idea.

"This is such hard work," she said, huffing and puffing.

"But I'm not going to help," said George.

"I'm getting tired," said Martha.

George had fun on the picnic.

"I'm so glad we came," said George.

But Martha wasn't listening.

She had fallen asleep.

STORY NUMBER FOUR

THE SCARY MOVIE!

Martha was nervous.

"I've never been to a scary movie before."

"Silly goose," said George. "*Everyone* likes scary movies."

"I hope I don't faint," said Martha.

Martha *liked* the scary movie. "This is fun," she giggled.

Martha noticed that George was hiding under his seat.

"I'm looking for my glasses," said George.

"You don't wear glasses," said Martha.

When the movie was over, George was as white as a sheet. "Hold my hand," George said to Martha. "I don't want you to be afraid walking home."

"Thank you," said Martha.

THE LAST STORY

THE SECRET CLUB

"Where are you going, George?" asked Martha.

"I'm going to my secret club," said George.

"I'll come along," said Martha.

"Oh no," said George, "it's a secret club."

"But you can let *me* in," said Martha.

"No I can't," said George. And he went on his way.

Martha was furious.

When George was inside his secret clubhouse, Martha made a terrible fuss.

"You let me in," she shouted.

"No," said George.

"Yes, yes," cried Martha.

"No, no," said George.

"I'm coming in whether you like it or *not*!" cried Martha.

When Martha saw the inside of George's clubhouse, she was so ashamed.

"You old sweetheart," she said to George.

George smiled. "I hope you've learned your lesson."

"I certainly have," said his friend.